The Adventures of
Titch & Mitch

The Adventures of
Titch & Mitch

Book 1
Shipwrecked!

Garth Edwards
Illustrated by Max Stasyuk

INSIDE
POCKET

Published in Great Britain by Inside Pocket Publishing Limited

First published in Great Britain in 2010

Text © Garth Edwards, 2009

Illustrations © Inside Pocket Publishing Limited

Titch and Mitch is a registered trade mark of Inside Pocket Publishing
Limited

A CIP catalogue record for this book is available from the British Library

ISBN 978-0-9562315-0-5

Inside Pocket Publishing Limited Reg. No. 06580097

Printed and bounds in Great Britain by CPI Bookmarque Ltd, Croydon

www.insidepocket.co.uk

For N & J

Contents

1

The Shipwreck

"NEVER LEAVE THE VALLEY!" SAID OLD
Master Wizzle, addressing a class of fifteen young
pixies. "It's dangerous out there, and you will be sure
to get lost." His wrinkled face had a little white beard
and blue eyes, which sparkled as he spoke. He was
old, small and loved to talk, especially about danger.
Many pixies had attended his classes over the years
and his pupils always listened intently to his tales of
the outside world.

But the trouble with Titch and Mitch was they
liked to explore. Of all the young pixies in Pixie
Valley, the two brothers were always the ones who
went missing or got stuck in the most unusual places.

As they left school, they were
already hatching a plan.

Early the next morning
they quickly made some
sandwiches, packed water
bottles and set out to
climb the steep hills that
surrounded the valley.
Titch was a year older
than his brother and
bolder. He was as tall as a
squirrel with curly brown
hair and blue eyes that
were full of energy. He was
always looking for
adventure. Mitch was the
shorter of the two, with a
cheerful face, and was
never seen without his
green woolly hat. The two
brothers were the best of
friends and very popular in the
valley of the pixies.

When they reached the top of the hillside and
looked around, they found they could see for miles.

Far in the distance the sea glistened in the early morning sun. However, it was when Titch leaned forward to search for a path down the other side that

disaster
struck.
The stone
he was
standing on
came loose and
tipped him over
the edge. He
grabbed his brother
to keep his balance
but it was too late.
Together they slipped and
both of them went
tumbling down the hillside.
Luckily, it was mostly grass
and loose stones but they went
head over heels, squealing and
shouting, until bruised and
battered they came to a stop on a
path at the bottom.

Standing up gingerly and checking that no bones
had been broken, the two pixies looked around them.
Unfortunately, they did not see the large fishing net
that came swishing out of the sky and scooped them
up off the ground. Once again, they were tumbling

around and when the net had them well and truly tangled up, they found themselves staring through the mesh at an ugly, spotty face.

By human standards, the face belonged to a

skinny, teenage boy, but by pixie standards, the boy was an ogre and the two brothers clutched each other in fright. They stared in horror at two black eyes, a spotty chin and limp dark hair that flopped over a pale forehead. When the creature spoke, its face twisted into a cruel smile.

"Ha, ha," it sniggered. "What strange little animals. Perfect specimens for my biology class." The two pixies had no idea what a biology class was, but they didn't like the sound of it.

The boy put the fishing net over his shoulder and, with Titch and Mitch dangling inside, he strode off along the path. Eventually they came to a seaside café where the boy grabbed the pixies in two very dirty hands and upended them into a cardboard box. After he had carefully removed the net, he placed a lid over the box, leaving the two brothers trapped inside.

"Oh dear," said Titch. "The ogre must have seen us tumble down the hillside. What are we going to do?"

"There's nothing we can do while we are trapped in here. Listen, what's the ogre saying?"

There were other children in the café and they wanted to know what was in the box.

"Never you mind," said the boy, "I have two weird little animals and I'm taking them back to school with me." He moved the box to one side away from his school friends.

"We must escape," said Titch. "I don't want to be part of a 'biology' class, whatever it is."

Mitch poked around the box and found it empty but old and dusty. In one corner, the cardboard was particularly worn. Mitch started to scrabble at it. He called to his brother, "Come quickly, I think we can make a hole in this part of the box."

After what seemed like an age, the two pixies made a small hole in the corner of the box and Mitch peeped out. Next to them and staring blankly into space was a large man with a black beard and wearing a thick, blue, roll-neck sweater. On the seat next to him lay a crumpled overcoat and a hefty sailor's kitbag, slightly open at the top.

Pulling himself back into the box, Mitch said, "Now's our chance, we can squeeze through the hole and hide under that big coat."

"All right, you go first," said his brother.

They made the hole a bit bigger then Mitch wriggled his way out and burrowed quickly under the coat. A few moments later Titch joined him.

After some careful wriggling around, Mitch whispered to Titch, "Follow me! I've found a bag and there's just enough room in it for both of us. If the big man leaves the cafe first then he'll take us with him and we'll escape from the horrid ogre."

The pixies had only just wriggled their way into

the kitbag when the big man stood up, put on his coat and slung the bag over his shoulder. "Duck down!" hissed Mitch to Titch, who was trying to peek out. "We don't want to be seen!" Titch and

Mitch were then carried along bouncing up and down in the kitbag with no idea of where they were going.

A short while later, the man stopped walking. Titch and Mitch stood up and peeped out of the kitbag. They were on a quay with a trawler right in front of them. It was a fishing boat, painted dark red with two short masts and a small cabin in the middle. Three of the crew were leaning over the side watching the new arrival. A voice called out from the boat. "Ahoy there, Captain, welcome aboard."

Above them, the pixies could hear seagulls calling, and they could smell salty air blowing on the breeze.

The big man threw his kitbag onto the boat and replied, "With a bit of luck we'll catch the evening tide and be fishing by morning."

"Perhaps we should wait awhile," said another sailor. "There's a storm brewing out in the west."

"Nonsense," replied the big man. "It won't bother us. This boat can cope with a storm."

The pixies ducked inside the bag and stayed there as the big man boarded the boat and entered his cabin. Once inside, he swung the bag off his shoulder and dumped it on the floor. A loud rumble announced the starting of the ship's engines. The captain took a deep breath, pulled open the door, and lumbered away down the corridor.

"Now's our chance," said Titch. "Let's get off this boat before it sails. We don't want to go on a fishing trip."

"I'm hungry," replied Mitch. "Can we find something to eat first?"

"No, we must hurry! Can't you hear the engines?"

Climbing out of the bag, the pixies inched their way through the open door and into the corridor. After making sure the passage was clear, they began to make their way up to the deck. But by the time they had scrambled up the stairs, they discovered to their horror that the fishing boat had already left the harbour and was heading out to open sea.

"Oh no," said Titch. "What are we going to do now?"

"Go and find something to eat," said Mitch. "Then we can find somewhere to hide. We might be on this boat for a long time."

After some careful exploration, they found an open door with the word 'GALLEY' written on it. Peering through the doorway they could see a small, narrow kitchen. There was nobody inside, so they went in and explored some more. Mitch found a tasty pork pie, a loaf of bread, a pot of jam, some trifle and a jug of milk. Titch found a cupboard with clean towels. In no time at all they were resting on the towels, snug and warm in the cupboard, surrounded by tasty food. After they had polished off the food, they made themselves comfortable and very soon fell asleep.

The screeching noise of a siren and a hideous rolling of the ship woke them up and they realised it was the middle of the night.

"What on earth is that?" shouted Mitch in fright.

"It's a storm. I just heard some thunder," replied Titch.

"What if the ship goes down with us trapped in this cupboard?"

"We must get up on deck and see what's happening."

However, every time they struggled to the door of the cupboard, the ship swayed over and they fell back down again. They had no way of getting out while they were being tossed around in the storm. Suddenly there was a savage shaking of the ship and a huge crashing noise. The cupboard door burst open and all the towels and the two pixies were flung out

onto the floor.

As they landed, they heard men outside shouting. One very loud voice roared, "ALL HANDS ON DECK! MAN THE LIFEBOAT! ABANDON SHIP!"

But Titch and Mitch couldn't abandon ship. Every time they stood up, they fell over again, so they sat on the floor clutching hold of each other in the dark and trembled in fright. Soon they could hear the engines of the lifeboat as it sped away.

"We've been left behind and we're going to drown," wailed Mitch. Titch said nothing.

Some time later the storm passed and the winds began to drop. The ship stopped rolling around and stayed almost still. Eventually daylight filtered in through the portholes and the pixies could see the debris and chaos the storm had caused in the galley. The cabin door hung open, so Titch and Mitch walked tentatively through into the passageway outside and climbed up the steps onto the deck. There was no sign of any of the crew and when the pixies looked over the side of the boat, they saw a large rock jutting out of the water. It seemed the

fishing boat had been blown off course by the storm and was now stuck firmly on this large, grey lump.

Gasping for breath, the two found themselves relieved to be alive but alarmed at the thought of being left alone in a shipwrecked boat with no sign of land.

"Let's look on the other side of the ship," suggested Mitch.

So they struggled across the deck and gazed out to sea. To their amazement and delight there was a small island just a short distance from the stranded boat.

"Look," cried Titch. "I can see a sandy beach. If we can reach it, we'll be saved."

"Let's go and see if we can find something that floats. Maybe when the wind drops we can paddle our way across."

It proved impossible for the pixies to find anything left on the deck because the sea had washed everything overboard. After a lot of searching, they found a wooden barrel stuck in a corner right at the front of the ship. It was dark and greasy, but seemed solid enough. Alongside it was a wooden post with enough foot-holes for them to climb up to the edge of the barrel and peer inside.

"Yuck," said Titch as he crinkled his nose. "It's got dead fish in the bottom. What a disgusting smell!"

Mitch leaned over the edge and sniffed as well. "We won't be going anywhere in that, I'm not sharing a barrel with a pile of dead fish."

At that moment, a huge grating sound sent shivers down their spines and the ship rocked back and forth. The tide was rising and finally the rock was loosening its hold on the fishing boat. With another jarring lurch, the boat slid heavily into the sea. The sudden jolt tipped the two brothers over the edge of the barrel and down to the bottom, where they landed on the pile of smelly fish.

"Ugh, ugh, ugh," gasped Titch in horror as he sat up on top of the fish.

"Yuck, yuck, yuck," roared Mitch as he also landed on the fish and tried to stand.

"Let's get out of here." Titch tried to climb the walls of the barrel but the sides were too high and too slippery so he fell down on the fish again and lay flat on his back.

In his hurry to escape from the barrel, Mitch stood on top of Titch.

"Yarroo!" spluttered Titch, as his brother's foot

squashed his face into a particularly smelly fish.

"Yoiks!" roared Mitch as he tried again to jump out of the barrel but slid back down the slippery walls and once more fell on top of his brother.

"Yarroo!" roared Titch again as his face was squashed back into the same reeking specimen.

There came the sound of rushing water and the two pixies went very quiet. Seconds later, the barrel

began to bob up and down and they realised that the ship had sunk and the barrel was floating free in the choppy sea. Despite the stinking fish, they counted their blessings; if they hadn't fallen into the barrel, they would have gone down with the ship.

They were still sitting glumly on top of the fish when the barrel washed up on the shore and tipped over onto its side. Titch and Mitch crawled out and before the next wave could rush in and pull them back into the sea, they managed to stagger clear of the water.

Sitting on the sand in warm sunshine they slowly dried off and looked around. The persistent screeching of the seagulls made them look up into the sky. There were so many seagulls they cast a shadow over the sun. One of the birds suddenly darted down and made them duck. Then another one dived down at them but swooped away at the last minute.

"Why are those birds diving at us?" said Titch in alarm.

"And what is that?" Mitch pointed at a creature walking towards them. It had a long twitching nose with many whiskers bristling on either side. Its flat head was low to the ground showing a long body covered with brown and white fur. Small, shiny, black eyes stared at them.

"I don't like the look of that," said Titch nervously. "I wish I was back at home."

As the creature came nearer, Mitch hissed, "It's a giant rat!"

The rat got so near that the two pixies were too frightened to move.

Coming to a halt, the rat gave them a curious look, then said, in an unexpectedly squeaky voice, "I say you two, would you mind awfully if I had a nibble of the fish in that barrel? Any minute now those seagulls will be in and scoff the lot."

To their great relief, the rat seemed more interested in the fish than in them.

"Who are you?" asked Mitch.

"I'm Willy the water rat," said the rat. "And I love fish."

Obligingly the pixies moved to one side and Willy the water rat walked into the barrel and, after some sniffing about, came out with a fish in his mouth.

"Thank you," he said through clenched teeth, and waved a paw at the brothers before wandering off.

As soon as he went, a great crowd of seagulls descended on the fish barrel and began to squabble over the tastiest portions.

Moving carefully away from the raucous birds, Titch and Mitch began to pick their way through the strewn debris from the shipwreck, which had washed up with them. There were planks of wood, tins of food, bundles of netting and piles of rope everywhere. Then they watched the water rat as he walked back

towards the cliffs.

A thought occurred to Mitch.

"That Willy creature might be a great help to us if he lives here and knows the island. Let's go and talk to him."

The two pixies raced up the beach after Willy and caught up with him as he settled down to eat his fish.

"Willy," said Mitch. "Will you tell us about the island?"

The water rat munched away at his fish for a while before answering in an amiable way, "It's a very pleasant place to live; there's water, and fish, which I like. What else do you want to know?"

"How big is it?" asked Titch.

"Do humans live here?" asked Mitch.

"Is there any fresh water?"

"Are there any cats or foxes here?"

"Are there any witches or trolls or goblins?"

Willy finished the last of his fish before standing up and ambling towards a path that led up the cliffs to the top of the island. He looked back at the pixies and said, "Come on, I'll show you around."

At the top of the cliffs, Willy walked through a meadow and with Titch and Mitch on either side, he chatted away. "It's a small island with cliffs all round and just this one tiny beach." He pointed towards a lot of trees and beyond it to a hill that rose high in the sky. "There's one hill over there, covered in trees. No humans live here. It really is a very small island, although the mainland is not far away, so I'm told. There are rabbits, badgers, squirrels, otters, plenty of birds, and, of course, some water rats."

They came to a clearing where a stream ran out of the wood and flowed gently over some rocks before twisting and turning its way through the meadow and down towards the cliffs. "I live in the bank of that stream," said Willy, his nose twitching. He turned to the pixies with a smile and a twinkle in his eyes. "You two smell just like a tasty piece of fish,"

he said, licking his greasy lips. "I am very tempted to eat you."

Titch and Mitch realised how smelly they must be after their adventures in the barrel, so they rushed down to the stream and jumped straight in. After scrubbing themselves clean, they sat down on the bank and rested in the warm sunshine.

Mitch said thoughtfully, "This might be a pleasant spot to stay for a while." He turned to his brother and added, "What do you think?"

"It not the same as pixie valley, but it looks very exciting. Yes, let's build a house here and make some friends."

At that moment, a large rabbit bounded out of the woods and sat close to them. He was a very strong looking rabbit with white tips to his long ears. Brown, friendly eyes smiled a welcome to the pixie brothers.

"That's Big Jack Rabbit," said Willy, by way of introduction, as a number of smaller rabbits ran up and joined him.

"Pleased to meet you," said Jack Rabbit in a gruff voice. "This is my family," and he waved at the bundle of small rabbits tumbling around his feet. The young rabbits then jumped around Titch and Mitch clamouring for attention and calling out questions in shrill voices.

"Where did you come from?"

"Do you eat grass?"

"Are you pixies or elves?"

"Can you climb trees?"

"My name is Tinker and I can run faster than anyone on the island," boasted the very smallest rabbit.

"Be Quiet!" called out Big Jack.

Titch and Mitch looked around in surprise and saw many red squirrels jumping from tree to tree, four hedgehogs snuffling in the undergrowth and two large badgers wandering up to meet them. In no time at all there was quite a crowd of small animals gathered around them, each one looking at them curiously. Willy stood up on his haunches and shouted out loudly, "Pay attention everyone! Allow me to introduce Titch and Mitch. They are pixies and thinking of staying on the island for a while."

The little rabbits and all the other animals cheered. "Hurrah, do stay here," they said in unison.

Titch stood up and said. "Thank you, we are going to build a house on this very spot."

The rabbits cheered again and Big Jack said, "We can all help you, just shout out and we'll come running."

Mitch turned to his brother and said. "The stuff on the beach! There were all sorts of things we could use to build a house."

Titch nodded in agreement. "Let's go and collect as much as we can before the tide washes it all out to sea again."

The pixies jumped up and headed back to the beach, followed by a host of small animals all eager to help.

By the time night came, they had built a shelter out of poles and a tarpaulin rescued from the beach.

Some towels, dried in the afternoon sun, made a pair of comfortable beds and the two brothers settled down to sleep.

"Tomorrow, we can start to build a proper house," said Mitch.

"Yes," agreed Titch, a big smile across his face. "I think we're going to like it here."

2

Budgie, The Yellow Seagull

BY THE SIDE OF A STREAM AT THE EDGE OF
a pleasant wood, Titch and Mitch built a neat little
house with a small garden surrounded by a low fence.
Various small creatures from the island helped them
to build it. The rabbits collected wood and items
from the beach where the pixies were shipwrecked.
The moles and the badgers used their sharp claws to
dig out the foundations and the squirrels joined in
fitting everything together. The two pixies loved their
new home on the island. Though very close to the
mainland, the island was hardly ever disturbed by
people, being so small and mostly surrounded by
cliffs.

Early one morning, Willy Water Rat came running up to the front gate puffing and muttering in a most agitated fashion. "Come quickly!" he called out to the pixies. "The hawk is back."

The two pixies had just finished breakfast when they heard their friend call out and rushed outside as fast as they could. They had heard stories about the hawk before.

"Where? Where is he?" said Mitch in a worried voice.

"Up there, up there," Willy sat back on his haunches and poked a paw up at the sky.

Sure enough, high in the sky and still only a dot in the distance, they could see it circling around. The hawk had keen, sharp eyes, a great curved beak and talons that could rip through flesh in an instant. He would circle in the sky while choosing which of  the island creatures he would have for his next meal, then drop like a stone and dive in for the kill. All the small animals and birds were terrified of him and

kept a close eye on the sky whenever the hawk was around.

As they watched the hawk circling above, they heard a thumping sound vibrating through the ground.

"Good," said Titch. "That sounds as though Big Jack Rabbit has seen him and the warning has gone out to all the rabbits." Big Jack was the oldest and heaviest of the rabbits and when his back legs started to thump on the ground like a drum, all the animals heard it.

"Look at them run," cried Mitch with delight. "That old hawk won't catch anyone today."

Sure enough, the little white tails of many rabbits were racing for the shelter of the thick wood. In amongst them lots of other little animals heeded the warning and they all raced for safety as fast as they could.

As they disappeared into the wood, Mitch clapped his hands with delight. "That's it, no breakfast for Old Hawk today."

They turned round to go back into the house when a shadow quickly passed over them. Looking upwards, they were horrified to see a seagull flying in off the sea. Immediately they shouted and waved at the seagull. "Go away, go away."

The seagull must have heard them and grown curious as it flew in a lazy circle, passing over them again.

"It's a yellow bird!" said Mitch. "I thought it was a seagull but I've never seen a yellow seagull before."

"It doesn't matter what it is," cried Titch. "It

shouldn't be here. Fly away, you silly bird."

Again, they waved their arms and shouted together. "The hawk, the hawk. He's right above you. Fly, fly, quickly."

Still curious, the yellow bird waggled its wings and soared down low right over them. Then it climbed high in the sky, put its head down, and did a complete somersault. Climbing high again, it did another somersault and zoomed back down towards them again.

"It's showing off," said a startled Mitch. "It can't hear us. It thinks we're just being friendly and waving a greeting.

"The hawk has seen it," said Titch in alarm.

High above, the hawk had stopped circling and looking for prey. He had found what he wanted right beneath him and now he hovered, a motionless dot in the sky. Then, as the pixies watched in horror, the hawk dropped and plunged downward as straight as an arrow towards the unsuspecting yellow bird.

With a final wiggle of its wings the yellow bird turned lazily towards the open meadow. Titch and Mitch were already racing after it when the hawk struck from above, instantly carrying the yellow bird straight down to the ground. Landing in a cloud of dust and feathers, the hawk regained its balance and, holding the yellow bird in one great claw, brought its head back so the curved beak could finish off its prey.

A sudden movement caught the hawk's eye and turning his head he saw the two wildest pixies in the world racing along the grass towards him. Their little legs were just a blur as they skimmed along to rescue the yellow seagull. The hawk became aware of a great roar from them as the two pixies ran straight for him.

Stepping aside from the injured yellow bird, the hawk, who did not intend to lose his breakfast, prepared to fight. Stretching his huge wings, he made himself look even bigger than he was and his dark eyes stared straight at the charging pixies. Suddenly, he became aware that they were not alone. Emboldened by the rush of the fearless brothers, Big Jack Rabbit had broken out from the wood and, together with a dozen of his biggest relations, he was charging along behind the two pixies and catching them up rapidly.

In amongst them, Willy Water Rat was snarling with rage and his entire family were with him, charging in support of Titch and Mitch. Even the youngest water rat, running well behind the rest, was snarling as best he could. Now this was suddenly a much more formidable foe than just the pixies alone.

As the charging horde got nearer, the hawk decided that he did not like the look of the great crowd of animals led by the two fierce looking pixies. It was all too much for him. The island was turning out to be a very dangerous place for a hungry hawk. He decided just in time to abandon his victim and get away to safety.

Leaping into the air and flapping his wings

violently, he almost got clean away, but not before Mitch, leaping higher than he ever thought possible, grabbed at the tail of the departing hawk with his outstretched hand and plucked out a single feather.

The hawk was now very relieved to get away and as he gained height, several smaller feathers fluttered gently to the ground where they were promptly seized upon as souvenirs by the younger rabbits.

Their jubilation was short lived. On the ground beside them lay the yellow bird, unconscious and bleeding from where the hawk's talons had gripped it so firmly. Mitch kneeled over the stricken bird and spoke softly to it.

"Are you alive? Can you hear me?"

To their relief one eye opened and blinked at Mitch. "What happened?" The voice was faint and weak.

"The hawk got you, while you were busy showing off. But don't worry we've chased him away. I don't think he'll come back in a hurry."

The rabbits and the water rats all cheered when they heard the bird speak. Their efforts to save him had not been in vain.

"We have to get this poor bird back to our house so we can patch it up and let it get some rest." Mitch

leaned over the yellow bird again and said, "What's your name? What type of bird are you?"

The voice was weak and pathetic. "I'm called Budgie and I'm a seagull."

"A seagull? But you're yellow. I've never seen a yellow seagull before." He looked at the rest of the crowd and they all nodded in confirmation. None of them had ever seen a yellow seagull either.

By now, the poor bird was too weak to respond so Titch called over Big Jack and asked if he could carry the bird on his back.

"No problem," he said. "Just lift her up and I'll wriggle underneath."

Everybody lent a hand and soon all the animals were helping the yellow bird stay upright on Jack's broad back as they walked slowly back to the cottage.

When they arrived at the little cottage, the two pixies managed to get the bird inside and placed her on the sofa.

"You're safe here," said Titch. "Just you rest a while and you'll soon get better."

He then turned round and shooed the rest of the animals out of the house, saying, "We must let poor Budgie recover. Come again tomorrow and see how she is."

By the evening, Budgie was feeling much better. She'd had some soup and Mitch had patched up all her wounds. "Thank you so much," she said. "I got such a shock when that hawk hit me. I had no idea he was anywhere nearby. They are so sneaky, hiding so high up and then pouncing on smaller creatures. I don't like hawks very much."

The bird turned her head to one side and little black eyes twinkled as she regarded Titch and Mitch quizzically. "Are you pixies? I've never seen a pixie before. How very strange."

"Yes, we are pixies," said Titch. "Just normal pixies and not in the least bit strange. This is Mitch and I am called Titch."

Mitch was intrigued by the bird's curious appearance. "How can you be a seagull when you're yellow all over?"

Titch laughed out loud. "You're obviously not a seagull, you're a giant budgerigar. That's why you are called Budgie."

"No, I am not!" protested the bird. "I'm a seagull."

"How long have you been yellow?"

"I don't like to talk about it. It's embarrassing."

"Go on," urged Mitch, whose curiosity was growing. "We won't tell anyone, I promise."

"Well, if you must know, I was watching some workmen repairing a road, when one of them dropped a sandwich. As soon as the coast was clear I swooped down to collect it. Unfortunately, the tarmac on the road hadn't quite hardened and I spent too long eating the sandwich. Then, when I came to fly away, I found that my feet were stuck fast in the road. I struggled and flapped as hard as I could but it was no good, I couldn't escape.

"Then a huge vehicle came along, a real monster, spitting fire and hissing steam and smelling awful. It came right at me and then right over me. I was sprayed with yellow paint and then savagely brushed

with a large, bristly wheel. I was lucky to be still alive when the vehicle had passed. Anyway, the dragging and scraping pulled my feet out of the tarmac and I was left lying dazed on the ground. I had become part of the yellow stripes down the side of the road."

The pixies laughed loud and long. For a while Budgie sulked, but she soon saw the funny side as well and joined in.

The following morning all the animals came round to see if Budgie was getting better. They were delighted to see her out of the house and running up and down practising for a take off.

To a great cheer, Budgie made a short, powerful run and flew off into the sky. She quickly gained height, waggled her wings to make sure they were working properly and then, with a little wave, zoomed off over the hill.

About an hour later, while Titch and Mitch were weeding in their garden, Budgie landed alongside them with a squawk. In her beak, she was holding a large, ripe plum. Dropping it at their feet she said, "I hope you like plums because while I was trying out my wings, I came across an old plum tree. It grows in the middle of a great thicket so I'll bet none of the animals knows it exits, and it's full of succulent

plums."

Titch and Mitch had never tasted plums before and had no idea that they grew on the island. With great excitement, they cut it in two and sucked and gobbled on the juicy fruit. It was delicious. "Thank you so much Budgie. This plum is delicious!" said Mitch.

"I've got an idea," said Titch. "Why don't we plant the plum stone in the garden and then maybe in a few years time we'll have our own plum tree."

"Good idea," responded Budgie. "And I'm so glad you like it. It's the least I can offer for saving my life.

And guess what else? After I toured the island and found the plum tree, I decided I would stay and build a nest on the cliffs nearest the beach." She pointed a wing downriver. "That's where I'm going to live from now on and I'll be able to do you a few more good turns in the future."

The two pixies clapped their hands with delight and invited Budgie inside for a cup of tea.

"Tomorrow," said Titch to Mitch as they walked into the house. "I suggest we go and find this plum tree. I want another one already."

3

The Magic Bicycle

A GREAT WIND HIT THE ISLAND ONE NIGHT and Titch and Mitch were woken by the sound of it howling through the trees in the nearby wood. It was all very frightening, but by the morning the wind had gone and the day was still and calm. Titch and Mitch, with nothing better to do, decided that they would go and look for the plum tree Budgie the yellow seagull had found on the hill in the centre of the island.

A journey up the hill could be quite a trek, so they packed their rucksacks with their favourite foods and a few other items they thought might come in handy. Then, after a hearty breakfast, they

recounted the instructions given to them by Budgie:
follow the stream where it flows down the hill, turn
right at the forked tree and you will see a little path
that goes right past the thicket that hides the plum
tree.

Around about mid-morning, the two pixies
stopped for a drink of water from the stream they
were following and to eat a snack of homemade
biscuits. As soon as they sat down on the grass they
heard a rustle from the undergrowth and the long
nose of Percy Hedgehog poked out. "I say you two,
what's that you're eating?" The nose reached out

towards the biscuit that Mitch was about to pop into his mouth and sniffed.

Quickly Mitch shoved the whole biscuit into his mouth, which then bulged so full he found he couldn't speak.

"Hello Percy," said Titch. "What are you doing out at this time of day. Aren't you supposed to be a creature of the night?"

"Oh I am, but last night was so windy, it took me twice as long to do everything I had to do. Then I stopped for a rest by this bush and fell asleep. Now I've just woken up and its morning already. I'm a bit hungry though." He directed his nose towards Mitch's rucksack and sniffed again.

Titch laughed. "Would you like a biscuit? Mitch made them you know, and they're jolly nice. We always pack too much to eat when we have a picnic. Why don't you sit down and join us?"

Percy responded immediately by emerging fully from the bushes and sitting down next to Titch. "Thank you most kindly, I do love a picnic."

The sun came out and it was very tempting to stop for a lot longer than they intended, but the thought of the delicious plums made Mitch impatient. "We must push on up the hill or we won't

get home until its dark," he insisted.

Reluctantly Titch agreed, so they said farewell to
Percy, who promptly rolled himself back into a ball
and went to sleep.

A short while later as they walked along the path,
Titch suddenly stopped in mid-stride. "What's that
noise?" he said. "I heard something call out."

They both stood still and listened intently. Sure
enough, there came a faint cry. "Help, help," it said,

then everything went silent.

"You're right," said Mitch. "I heard a cry for help, but where did it come from?"

"Over there." Titch seemed certain and he pointed towards a large bush in the distance.

They rushed over to the bush. It turned out to be a very thick bramble, all thorns and prickles. They stopped to listen again and from the middle of the bush came the thin cry once more.

"Help me, please."

"We're here," called out Titch. "Where are you?"

"In amongst the brambles. I'm stuck and my wings are caught up in the thorns."

They looked very hard into the

bramble bush. Right in the middle they could see a small, delicate figure with her arms, legs and wings all tangled up with the brambles.

"A fairy!" said Mitch, quite astounded.

"Gosh!" said Titch. Neither of them had ever seen a fairy so close up before.

"Oh dear," she wailed. "The more I struggle the worse it gets. I'll never get away. I'll be here forever."

"No you won't. We'll rescue you!" cried Titch.

The two pixies grabbed some nearby sticks and slashed at the brambles in an effort to break through, but try as they might they couldn't get very far. Soon they had to stop for a rest.

"It's no good," said Mitch panting with the effort. "Our sticks aren't big enough and the brambles are too thick."

"We need something heavy so we can squash the brambles and make a path."

"We don't have anything!"

The sound of sobbing came from the middle of the bush. The fairy had heard them talking and she was now crying because they couldn't get her out.

"Wait a minute," said Mitch. "I have an idea. There's quite a slope right behind us. If we can roll a large, heavy ball down that hill it will crash into the bush and make a path."

"Brilliant…" replied Titch sarcastically. "Where do we find a heavy ball and how would we get it up that hill."

"Percy Hedgehog!" shouted Mitch. "He could do it."

"Of course!" Titch clapped his hands with delight. "He can curl himself into a ball and roll down the hill. We must be quick though, he's having a nap right now, but if he wakes up and moves on we'll

never find him."

"You're the faster runner, Titch. You go."

Mitch was right, so as quick as he could Titch went racing down the path to the spot where they had had their snack and left Percy Hedgehog snoozing in the sun.

Meanwhile Mitch tried hard to keep up the fairy's spirits by chatting to her. "Don't worry fairy, we'll soon have you out of there. By the way, what's your name? And how did you get stuck in those brambles anyway?"

"Misty is my name. I was blown off course by that huge wind last night and before I knew it, here I was, trapped. I don't even know where I am!"

"You poor thing, if you've been stuck there all night. You must be exhausted."

"I am. Terribly so. Oh, please don't leave me here."

"Of course not, we'll find a way to get you out. I just hope we can find Percy."

A short while later Mitch saw Titch staggering back up the path and right behind him, running as fast as his little legs would go, was Percy Hedgehog.

"Hurrah," cried out Mitch to Misty. "Here they come, and Titch has brought Percy."

Percy looked at the bramble hedge and then looked at Titch and Mitch. "You actually think that I can batter my way through all those brambles and make a path into the middle. You must be crackers! I'll be torn to shreds."

In the middle of the bush, the fairy started sobbing again.

Mitch explained. "Of course you can do it. All you need to do is to climb a little way up this hill and curl yourself into a tight ball and then roll down and crash into the bush."

Percy looked doubtful.

"When you curl yourself into a ball, the sharpest teeth of the biggest fox in the whole world can't reach you. Surely a few prickles from a bramble bush won't be a problem."

Percy was keen to help so he said, "Oh alright then, I'll try, but one of you will have to start me rolling down the hill; when I've curled up tight I can't move."

"I'll do that," said Titch.

So, Titch and Percy climbed up the slope and Titch found a stick with which to prod Percy and make him roll. Finally, Percy said, "This spot should be about right." Curling himself into an extra tight ball with all his spines sticking out he called, "I'm ready."

Titch walked around Percy until he found the right spot and took careful aim at the bramble bush below them. "Ready, steady, go!" he shouted loudly and gently poked Percy with his stick. From inside the ball of strong spines came a yelp. Then the ball started rolling down the hill. Slowly at first and then, as the slope got steeper, the ball rolled faster and faster. Finally it crashed into the bramble bush and rolled right into the middle of it.

"Hurrah," cried Mitch. "You've done it." He followed Percy into the bush along the path he had made. By the time he got into the middle of it, Percy had straightened himself out very carefully and was inching his way back out of the brambles. So Mitch used his stick to beat at the thorns to help Percy back out.

Eventually they retreated out of the bush and Percy said, "See, no problem. I knew I could do it."

"Well done," said Titch and Mitch together.

The two pixies went back into the bramble bush and carefully released the fairy from all the thorns and prickles. Between the two of them they carried Misty to safety and laid her down on the grass.

"Oh, thank you so much," she said, and threw her arms around each of them in turn and gave them a big hug. Percy also got a special big hug for being so brave, but she was careful not to go too near his spines. Misty had had enough of prickly things for one day.

Finding she could walk all right, the four of them went back down the hill to the stream where they all had a drink of clear, fresh water. Titch and Mitch then gave the rest of their packed lunch to Misty who was very hungry after spending all night in the bramble bush.

They examined the fairy's thin wings for any damage, which took a long time, as it was most important she didn't find any holes in them when she was flying across the sea.

"Where do you live?" asked Percy Hedgehog. "I've never seen a fairy on this island before."

"Well, I don't know where I live right now. I was blown off course. I'm very lucky to have landed on this island." She shuddered at the thought of being swept out to sea. "Fairies never go flying in a wind you know, even a little breeze can be difficult. I was visiting friends yesterday when the wind started and I thought, 'Oh good, it will blow me home even faster', but I was very wrong, the wind was so strong I was blown right over my home and out across the water."

"How will you find your way back?"

"So long as there is no wind, I fly high in the air, look for the mountain with the white cloud around it and then head for that. As soon as I fly over a river next to a wide road I know where I am. Then, it's down to the crooked tree and into our secret valley."

"Do you live on your own?"

"All these questions," said Misty laughing happily. "No, there are a lot of fairies in the valley. One day you must come and visit us, and I can tell everyone what heroes my pixie friends are."

"We'd love to," added Titch, "but pixies don't have wings."

Looking anxiously at the sky Misty said, "I really must be on my way, but before I go I must give you a present." For a moment she looked thoughtful and then clapped her hands. "Oh yes, I know what I'll give you. Where do you live?"

Percy said quickly, "Under a hawthorn bush at the bottom of the hill. It's the one near the oak tree..." But Titch silenced him and, shaking his head, said, "There's no need to reward us. We enjoyed helping you."

"But you must come and visit us some time", Mitch added. "We have a little house, next to the stream, at the bottom of the hill."

"Well, I'll say goodbye now." Misty fluttered her wings. "When you get home, remember the magic words: Up, up and away."

Jumping up and down a few times Misty tested her wings. Then, with a final leap, she took off, and flew higher and higher in the sky until she was no more than a small dot in the distance.

"I wonder what she meant by magic words," wondered Titch.

"I'm sure I don't know," said Mitch. "We'd better go home now. I've had enough adventure for one day.

Those tasty plums will have to wait until tomorrow."

"Yes," said Percy. "I'm supposed to be asleep all day. That roll down the hill has quite exhausted me. I'm off as well."

After saying goodbye to the weary hedgehog, the two brothers made their way down to the bottom of the hill and followed the stream back to their little cottage. Approaching the garden gate, they came to a sudden stop. Standing in the centre of the lawn was a gleaming new bicycle. Astounded, they approached it, dazzled by it's shiny, silver paintwork. Tied to the handlebar with a red ribbon was a note. Titch looked at it and read it out loud – 'Thank you for your help. Remember the magic words. With love from Misty.'

The two pixies were astonished. It was a lovely bicycle, though it looked as light as a feather and had two little blue seats so they could sit one behind the other.

"Oh, let's try it out," said Mitch.

Titch jumped on to the front seat and took hold of the handlebars. Mitch jumped on to the seat behind him, put his arms round Titch's waist and said, "Now what?"

Titch pedalled as hard as he could and the bicycle wobbled around the garden.

"Try the magic words," suggested Mitch.

"Up, up and away," shouted Titch.

Immediately the bicycle shot straight up into the air and in no time at all they were wobbling right over their house.

"Put it down," screamed Mitch. "I'm frightened."

"I think I know what to do," called back Titch. Grasping the handlebars tightly, he made the bicycle zoom around the house a couple of times, then he went high up in the air before floating gently back down to the garden.

"This is fantastic," he said, leaping off his seat and doing cartwheels round and round the garden. He turned to Mitch. "We can go all over the place now, even over the sea to the mainland. We can go and explore the rest of the world. Three cheers for Misty!"

"Let's go somewhere now," cried Mitch in delight. "Let's go on the bicycle to get the plums."

Titch agreed and the two pixies jumped back on their new bicycle and together they shouted, "Up, up and away."

Again, they shot up into the air. With Titch steering, they headed up the hill until they came to the great tangled thicket Budgie had described.

"There it is!" shouted Mitch.

Sure enough, in the middle of the thicket stood an old plum tree, fully laden with ripe, juicy plums. Easing the magic bicycle down beside it, the two friends dismounted and then climbed into the plum tree's lower branches. They picked as many of the lovely, purple plums as they could carry, before returning to their bicycle and taking off again for the homeward journey.

That night, two very happy pixies polished off their dinner with a very tasty plum crumble.

4

Wiffen, The Intelligent Turkey

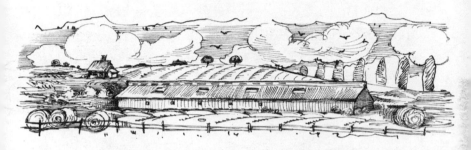

IT WAS A VERY FINE AND SUNNY MORNING
when Budgie, the yellow seagull, came to visit Titch
and Mitch. She sat on their sofa and told them
stories about her visits over to the mainland and
soon they wanted to go and explore the land she
talked about.

They had been keen to use the magic bicycle that
Misty the fairy had given them to fly the short
distance to the mainland. Budgie told them to avoid
all the places where human people lived because it
could be awkward to land right amongst them. "Oh
and by the way," she said, "don't land on a road.
They are the worst places in the world and very

dangerous."

Titch said, "Shall we go and visit Misty? She gave us directions to find the secret valley where the fairies live and said we could go and visit her any time."

"Oh Titch," said Mitch with great excitement, "I'd love to visit the Valley of the Fairies. Let's go today."

"OK, you make a picnic and I'll get the bicycle out."

By mid-day the two pixies were sitting on their magic bicycle ready to set off. Titch was sitting at the front planning the route, and Mitch sat behind, wearing his pointed green hat adorned with the long hawk's feather. After final checks that everything was secure, they called out together, "Up, up and away."

The bicycle soared into the air and with Mitch clutching Titch around the waist they set off across the sea. The journey thrilled them. They had never flown so high in the sky before and when they arrived over land they looked down to see fields, woods and the houses where the human people lived. They were joined on the journey by lots of very curious birds flying all around them. Some came far too close and made the pixies nervous.

"Shoo," called out Titch as a very large seagull

brushed against the handlebars with the tip of its wings and made the bicycle wobble.

Realising that the two strange pilots had no food to give them, the birds got bored giving chase and soon left them alone to marvel at the new and unexpected sights on the ground.

"I'm hungry," said Mitch after a while, "Can we stop soon and have some lunch?"

"Sure, let's find a nice quiet spot," replied Titch.

Mitch looked down and spotted a large building with a long, flat roof. "Oh, let's stop on that roof. It should be safe there."

Titch zoomed down and landed on the roof alongside a square window, which was slightly open.

The first thing the two pixies did was to go and peep through the window. They were astonished to see lots and lots of turkeys of various sizes milling around inside.

Titch looked at Mitch with a puzzled expression on his face. "Why are so many turkeys all squashed up together in one enormous shed?"

"I don't know," shrugged Mitch. "It's the middle of the afternoon. Why don't they pop out for a play or a fly around?"

They peered through the window again. "They've

got wings but none of them are flying," said Titch. "Maybe they can't get out."

Sitting down at the edge of the roof, they started to eat their sandwiches and think about all those trapped turkeys, when suddenly there was a loud clatter on the window from the inside of the shed. Both of the pixies jumped up in the air at the noise. "What's that?" cried Mitch.

They ran to the open part of the window and found a turkey struggling to get out through the tiny gap. It was far too big to squeeze through the narrow opening and eventually it stopped flapping. As it fell away from the window, they heard it call out, "Open the window. I'll be back."

It was quite a struggle but eventually they stood either side of the narrow opening and with their arms outstretched, they heaved the window open a few more inches.

"What now?" said Titch, "I can't keep this up for long."

He didn't have to wait long, almost immediately the same turkey appeared and flew straight at the new, bigger opening and for a moment it got stuck again. There was a lot of flapping and a lot of squawking then finally, with a big effort, the turkey

popped out through the gap and landed at their feet.

"Hurrah!" shouted the turkey. "I'm out, I'm out, I'm out." It danced around them a few times and finally stopped to get its breath back and looked at them closely.

"Hey, you look just like human people, but so much smaller. Who are you?"

"We are pixies," said Mitch. "We haven't seen many human people. Do you know any?"

"Indeed I do. There are some over there in a big house. They own this turkey farm." He waved the tip of his wing vaguely in the direction of a house they'd noticed on their way in to land. "There's one I call Blob. He keeps the turkeys locked up all the time."

"Oh my goodness," said Mitch horrified. "Shall we open the window again and let them all out."

"A waste of time. They wouldn't bother. That lot wouldn't move anywhere away from all that food. All they do all day is eat, drink, eat, drink, and then they do it all over again."

"Why did you get out then? Aren't you the same as they are?"

The turkey puffed out his chest, raised his head up high and said, in a very important sounding voice, "I should think not! My name is Wiffen and I am the most intelligent turkey in the whole, wide world."

"How do you know that?" Titch was curious.

"Because I have spent my entire life in this huge shed with hundreds of other turkeys. Hardly any of them can speak at all, and those that do only say, 'Gobble, gobble, gobble.' I've tried to communicate with them, but it's a waste of time. They just peck at the ground and eat and then peck at the ground again. If there's anything on the ground, they peck it. It really is

soul destroying, but thanks to you two beautiful little pixies, I'm out and I'm not going back."

"Don't you have any friends down there?" Titch pointed to the window behind them.

"I certainly do not. Mind you, there is a guard dog called Perry. He's a good friend. Every night he sneaks into the shed to keep warm and sleeps by the inside door which is always kept locked by Blob. I sleep with all those turkeys on the other side of that door and sometimes we chat away right through the night."

Wiffen stretched his wings and made all his feathers stick straight out. He was bigger than the two pixies with a bright red wattle and beady eyes that blinked furiously when he was excited. On the top of his head there was a ring of small, white feathers that looked as if he wore a crown. He strutted along the edge of the roof and looked all around him.

"I wonder where I shall go to live. I suppose I could go anywhere in the world."

"How far can you fly?" asked Mitch, doubtfully.

"I don't know. I haven't been anywhere."

Peering over the edge of the roof, Wiffen said, "Oh look, I can see Perry. He's right down there."

Waving a wing, he called out, "Hi Perry, look at me, I'm up here!"

Titch and Mitch looked over the edge of the roof and there below was a large Old English sheepdog sitting on the ground beneath them.

Just at that moment, a man came round the corner of the shed. He was a short fat man with a red face and a bushy, black moustache. In his thick, hairy arms he carried a bale of hay.

Wiffen squawked and with his eyes blinking furiously said, "That's him. That's Blob. Don't let him see me." He jumped up in the air and lost his balance. For a while, he danced along the side of the roof flapping his wings then, with an even louder squawk, he fell right over the edge.

Titch and Mitch rushed to grab him but it was too late. Wiffen flapped and squawked all the way to the ground.

"Fly!" The two pixies shouted encouragement to the frightened bird as they watched him plummet.

It was lucky for Wiffen, but not so lucky for Perry, that the turkey landed on the unsuspecting guard dog.

Perry yelped with surprise and ran away as fast as he could, sending Wiffen tumbling in the dust.

The man called Blob dropped his bale of hay and rushed towards Wiffen with his hands outstretched and shouting furiously. As soon as Wiffen got to his feet and saw Blob almost on top of him, he shrieked with fright and ran away. Helped by flapping wings he managed to stay in front of the red-faced man, but although he tried very hard, he couldn't fly up into the air to escape.

The terrified turkey ran round the corner of the shed and disappeared from view. Titch and Mitch raced across the roof to the other side and saw him running between the shed wall and a rusty wire fence. Shouting down to Wiffen, they tried hard to give him encouragement. "Run! Fly! Go faster!"

Blob soon ran out of breath, turned round and called out to Perry. "Come here you horrible dog. You're supposed to be a guard dog. Get after that turkey and bring it back here."

The long-haired sheep dog took up the chase, and

the two pixies watched as Wiffen raced out into a lane with his wings flapping and his feet stamping the ground madly. Sometimes he was flying with his feet just off the ground and sometimes he was running with tired wings drooping along in the dust. Finally, Wiffen crashed straight through a rickety fence, sending a shower of splinters flying through the air. Still giving chase, Perry dashed through the hole after him.

"Come on Mitch," said Titch excitedly. "Let's go and help Wiffen. That dog will soon catch him up!"

Jumping on their bicycle, they called out the magic words, "Up, up and away!"

Immediately they were up in the air and, with Titch steering, they chased after the two creatures now racing off into the distance.

Making the bicycle skim low over the ground they followed the trail left by the turkey and the dog. Eventually they hopped over a hedge and there beneath them was Wiffen, sitting on the ground with his wings stretched out, his legs apart and leaning against the trunk of a tree. Alongside him, and gasping for breath, was Perry, who lay on his side in a state of complete exhaustion.

After hovering a few moments they gently landed

close by, but Perry made them nervous so they kept their distance. After all, compared to the pixies, the dog was huge and looked rather fierce. They stayed on their bicycle and called to Wiffen, "Are you all right?"

Wiffen gulped a few times, blinked and said, "I'm worn out. Some flying practice is needed. But I'm out of that place at least, and I'm not going back."

The two pixies stared at Perry anxiously. The big dog cocked his head on one side, looked at Wiffen with big, brown eyes and said in a deep voice, "And neither am I."

"That's right Perry, you stick with me. With my brains and your muscle, or rather your big teeth, we can take on anybody." Wiffen got to his feet and started to preen himself again.

"Where will you live?" asked Mitch, being ever so practical.

"Err, let me think now." Wiffen frowned and blinked his beady eyes. "First of all we need to have somewhere dry and sheltered were we can sleep safely. Then we need to have water nearby so we can drink whenever we want. And of course we need to have food. I'm used to lots of food you know."

There was silence as all of them considered the problem.

At last, Perry said, "I know where there's a bin at the back of the farm where lots of food gets thrown out by the people who live there. But it does have a lid on it."

"A lid!" exclaimed Wiffen. "I'll soon have the lid off. It can't be that difficult. We'll need a bag to carry the food in though."

"We can find you a bag," said Titch.

Looking at them thoughtfully, Wiffen said, "We need a view from the air to see what's around here. Unfortunately, I can't fly very well just yet, although I will be able to one day. I just need some practice. So if you very kind pixies were to fly around on your bicycle and have a look for somewhere nice to live, while Perry and I get our breath back, we would be very grateful." He smiled cheerfully at the two friends.

The pixies looked at each other and nodded in agreement. "All right. It's best we leave you somewhere safe, I suppose," said Titch.

Zooming up into the sky again they started to fly around in ever increasing circles with Titch steering and Mitch looking keenly at the ground beneath them.

"Hey Mitch," said Titch after a while. "Look over there, in the woods. It looks like an old stone cottage. Half of it has fallen down. Let's go lower and see if anyone lives there."

Making the bicycle hover right over the old cottage, they studied the ground all around it. There was no sign of any creatures living there at all, so Titch landed the bicycle just in front of the cottage and they both went in to explore.

There was one room with a roof on it. "That's a great bedroom," said Mitch. "Wiffen will be safe there, especially if Perry sleeps in the doorway to protect him."

Titch nodded, "They might be an odd couple, but Wiffen is right, a big dog and an intelligent turkey

could
make a good
team, especially if
Wiffen ever learns to fly."

"Yes, and look," added
Mitch, pointing behind the
cottage. "There's a stream
close by, and we can't be
that far away from the farm
so each day they can go and
look for something to eat.
Let's go and tell them."

Soon they were back
with Wiffen and Perry,
telling their new friends

all about the old, stone cottage they had found.

"Great," said Wiffen, "show us the way. You fly straight to it, and we'll follow on the ground."

Again, Titch and Mitch took to the air and headed off. Looking down they saw Perry running beneath them. On his back sat Wiffen, with both his wings wrapped tightly around the dog's neck and his claws gripping Perry's fur coat tightly. "Slow down you great, big dog. You'll shake me off," they heard him calling out as Perry bounded along the road.

When they landed at the cottage and showed the dog and the turkey what they had found, Wiffen was delighted. "This is a great place to live. It's got everything we need," he said with great enthusiasm. "We can bring some hay up from one of the farms around here to make it nice and comfy. Nobody will ever find us and we can go wherever we want."

"Thank you, Titch and Mitch," said Perry. "You must come and visit us in the future. Please promise you will."

"Of course we will," said Mitch. "We'll come as often as we can. But we must be on our way now if we are going to find Misty before night time."

"I need one more favour from you," Wiffen said anxiously. "Please find out when Christmas is, because I believe that is the time when intelligent turkeys go into hiding."

5

The Dragon Mouse

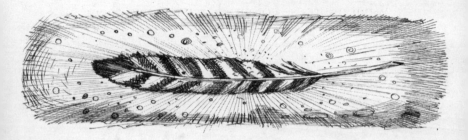

WIFFEN, THE INTELLIGENT TURKEY, AND HIS
friend Perry waved to Titch and Mitch as they soared
into the air on their magic bicycle and headed
towards the setting sun in search of Misty, their fairy
friend. This would be their first visit to her home.

It was getting very near to the end of the day
when Mitch, peering over Titch's shoulder, spotted
the crooked tree, which showed the way to the secret
valley where the fairies lived. They zoomed right over
it and carried on, following Misty's detailed
directions.

They went up a small hill then over the brow and
suddenly a deep valley appeared in front of them.

They could see lots of clouds beneath them as they floated gently down. When they reached the clouds, they found that they could see right through them and below was a beautiful, green valley with lots and lots of brightly coloured shapes on the ground.

"What are those coloured things down there?"

asked Titch as he leaned over the handlebars and tried to get a better view.

"I don't know," replied Mitch. "We need to get a bit closer."

Just then, a fairy appeared out of the clouds and flew very close. She had pale yellow wings and waved happily to them. As they neared the ground, they realised that there were many fairies flying around, all with different coloured wings. As they fluttered and dived about, it looked as though they were part of a shifting and shimmering rainbow.

Landing gently on the grass they dismounted from the bicycle and looked around in wonder. The coloured shapes they had seen turned out to be tents. The nearest one was very pale blue and, like the rest, perfectly round. Peeping out of the blue tent was a fairy with a pretty face and pale blue wings.

"Hello," she said. "Can I help you?"

"Oh yes please," replied Mitch. "We're looking for a fairy called Misty. Do you know her?"

"Yes, I know Misty. Her full name is Misty White and my name is Jane Blue." She lowered her voice and looked quite sad, "I hear she's not very well at the moment." The blue fairy pointed vaguely behind her. "She lives over there. "Misty has white wings, so

you need to find a tent which is white. Very simple really, all the fairies live in tents that are the same colour as their wings. Nobody can get lost in the Valley of the Fairies." Jane Blue tilted her head to one side, smiled and gave a little bob. "Goodbye. Come and visit me whenever you like."

They spotted a white tent very quickly, behind a

blue tent and next to a yellow one. Standing outside they looked around for a doorbell or something to knock on before entering.

"How can you knock on the door of a tent?" said Mitch, looking confused.

Just then, they heard a voice coming from inside the tent. It sounded like Misty but it was very weak and feeble. "Come in. Is that Titch and Mitch? I'm sure I can recognize your voices. Nobody needs to knock on doors in Fairy Valley"

Entering into Misty's home, the two brothers were surprised to see her lying in bed with her face covered in red spots. Immediately they were most concerned for their friend.

"What's the matter?" said Mitch.

"I've got chickenpox," croaked Misty. "Thank you for coming to see me."

"Is there anything we can do to help?" asked Titch anxiously.

"Oh, yes please, there is actually. I am very worried about a friend of mine. Have you ever met a dragon mouse?"

"No," said Titch. "What's a dragon mouse?"

"A dragon mouse is a bit bigger than an ordinary mouse and covered in scales. He breathes fire, like the very big dragons, so he's called a dragon mouse because he's really a very little dragon. His name is Trusty and he lives in a cave in the hills behind our valley. Poor Trusty needs my help."

"Why?" Mitch was keen to help their friend.

Misty carried on explaining, "Trusty lives in a dark cave and nearby is a strange pool which dragon mice drink from. This makes a dragon mouse breathe fumes that they can ignite and this causes the fire to leap out of their mouths. It is very dark in the cave, so Trusty needs to be able to breathe fire to light up his cave and keep warm. But poor Trusty has broken a tooth and until it's glued back again he can't breathe fire. You see, he needs to gnash his teeth together to light up his fiery breath. Will you pop over to see Trusty and give him this glue for his tooth? It's a special glue I've made for him."

"Of course we will," said Titch. "We'd be pleased to help."

"None of the fairies will come in and see me because of my chickenpox, but it's a fairy chickenpox and pixies can't catch it. I'm so glad you'll help."

Misty went quiet for a moment and then said, "You'll need light to see in that cave. Trusty is too timid to come out without his fiery breath. Mitch, will you let me have that hawk's feather you wear in your hat."

Mitch took the feather out of his hat and handed it over to Misty.

"Now," said Misty, "I'm going to make a spell for the feather." Holding the feather in her hands, she gently blew on it and sang out, "Little breath of Misty White. Let this feather share your light!"

Handing it back to Mitch, she said, "This feather will light up when you wave it gently over your head. If you point it straight out and waggle it as fast as you can, the light sparkles. That'll frighten creatures so much, they'll run away."

Mitch held the feather gently in his hand and looked at it in wonder.

"Now it's getting late. You must stay the night with me here in my tent and tomorrow, after a good rest, you can use the magic bicycle to go and help Trusty the dragon mouse."

The next day Titch and Mitch sat on their bicycle and Misty gave them the special glue in a little pouch, which Mitch tied firmly round his waist.

"Goodbye, Misty," they cried and with Titch steering the bicycle, the two brothers zoomed into the air and headed for the hills behind the valley.

Flying carefully and watching out for a cave near the top of the hill, the two pixies started the search. Titch spotted it first. "There, I can see it! It's between some trees and just a short

walk from the top of the hill."

"Let's land on the top then and walk down to the cave," suggested Mitch.

After they landed on a flat area of grass, they were walking down the slope to the cave, chatting happily, when Mitch suddenly stopped. "I can hear voices," he said. "Listen."

They tiptoed down to the edge of the cave and peeped round the corner. In front of the cave and sitting on a flat rock were three wild cats. They were looking into the entrance of the cave and calling out to Trusty.

One was a dirty looking, black cat with cold, green eyes who shouted out loudly, "Come out dragon mouse. You can't stay in there forever. We're very hungry and we feel like dragon mouse pie." The other cats squealed with laughter.

A very big, ginger cat was nearest to the two pixies. He had yellow eyes and a tail that waved from side to side and he joined in the taunting of Trusty by shouting, "Show us how brave you are without your fire, dragon mouse." This produced more laughter from the other cats.

Mitch whispered softly to Titch, "Poor Trusty, what are we going to do?"

"We must do something quickly. He must be terrified in there, as well as being hungry and thirsty. I know!" Picking up a stone that lay by his feet, Titch weighed it in his hands. "If we throw this stone so that it lands behind the cats, it might distract them. As soon as the cats turn round to investigate, we run as fast as we can into the cave."

"Good idea," said Mitch, "but I'm too frightened to move."

"We have to help Trusty. Are you ready?"

"Yes, I suppose so." Mitch's voice was very shaky.

Giving a great heave with his arm, Titch threw the stone as far as he could. It sailed over the heads of the cats and landed with a great thud right in the middle of a thorn bush. Startled, the cats all turned round together, their tails up, their fur bristling and their noses twitching as they tried to locate the source of the noise. Whilst they were looking away, Titch and Mitch raced around the side of the cave and darted in through the entrance. As they disappeared into the darkness, they heard howls of rage behind them.

The two brothers clutched at each other in the

blackness and trembled with fright, both unsure
which way to turn next. They had angry cats behind
them and a frightened dragon mouse somewhere in
front of them.

Plucking up his courage, Mitch tiptoed slowly into
the cave and called out bravely, "Are you there

Trusty? We are pixies and friends of Misty the fairy."

Titch nudged Mitch and whispered, "Try the hawk's feather."

Taking the feather out of his hat, Mitch waved it gently in the air. Immediately a bright light glowed all along the length of the feather and the cave lit up to reveal two little eyes gleaming in a corner at the back of the cave.

Moving towards the bright eyes, Titch said, "We've come to help you. Misty has got chickenpox

and she asked us to bring you some special glue for your tooth."

The dragon mouse eyed them suspiciously for a moment.

"Thank goodness for that," he said at last, in a low, gruff voice and came forward to meet them. When he stepped into the light, they saw a creature about the same size as Mitch and resembling a large mouse, although his whiskers were a bit short and stubby. He had sharp, pointy ears and, instead of fur, he had tiny scales all over his body. In fact, he was quite a fierce looking dragon in a very tiny way.

"There are three very horrid looking cats outside," said Titch. "What do they want?"

"They know I've lost my fire and they think I'm easy prey for hungry cats. Luckily they are too afraid to come into my cave, so they sit around outside hoping that soon I'll have to come out."

"Can we help you glue back your tooth?"

"Yes please, it's over here." Trusty took a small bag from a shelf at the back of the cave and opened it up. Taking out the tooth he gave it to Titch, then sat back on his haunches and opened his mouth.

Mitch held the feather close to Trusty's mouth to light it up brightly while Titch smeared glue all over the tooth and carefully placed it in the hole where it

belonged. "There we are," said Titch in triumph. "The tooth is back and it looks great. How does it feel?"

"Fine, very fine," said Trusty, moving his jaw from right to left to test out his newly replaced tooth. "Just give me a minute, then I'll give those cats what they least expect. I'll show them I've got my fire back."

Trusty stood up and prowled around the cave a few times. "Excuse me," he said to the pixies. "I just want to practice my roar." After a long drink from a cup of water, he snarled then suddenly let out a deep rumbling roar. "Roarrr." The two brothers jumped up in the air with surprise. It certainly was a most frightening roar.

"A magnificent roar," said Mitch with delight. "That'll frighten anybody."

"Let me just test my new tooth." Trusty lifted his chin and gently rubbed his teeth together. "Yes, I do believe I can gnash my teeth most effectively. Those cats are in for a big surprise. Stand behind me pixies, I'm ready to go."

Moving to the entrance of the cave, Trusty stood straight up and looked out at the cats. They saw him coming and hooted with delight.

"Where's your fiery breath then dragon mouse?" The ginger cat sneered.

"Shall we eat you roasted or shall we eat

you 'raw'?" The black cat said, and all three cats laughed raucously.

Suddenly, Trusty roared and pounded out of the cave running straight at the cats. They sat back on their haunches and looked at him in amazement. Trusty stopped, took a deep breath, gnashed his teeth and roared again. This time a great flame leaped out of his mouth and scorched the cats' whiskers. All three of them leapt up into the air with surprise, then backed away spitting and snarling in fury. They stared in horror at the fierce looking dragon mouse as he took another deep breath and gnashed his teeth loudly. Another flame and an ear-splitting roar came out of Trusty's mouth and with a screech and a loud meow the cats went tumbling down the side of the hill with their whiskers and tails smouldering.

"Hurrah," cried Mitch.

"Well done," yelled Titch. "They won't be back in a hurry."

As it was lunchtime the two pixies stayed to have some food with Trusty. They had some fried eggs and some roasted nuts and lots of tea and cake. Of course, they cooked on a campfire that Trusty lit with a gentle puff and a gnash of his teeth.

It was quite late in the day when the two pixies

said goodbye to their new friend and made their way back up the hill to the magic bicycle. As they came over the brow of the hill, they were still chattering away and laughing as they remembered the look on the faces of the cats as they fled away from Trusty.

However, they stopped dead in their tracks as they
looked up and saw the two black cats walking around
their bicycle and the big, ginger cat sitting on the
front seat and looking at them with a wicked smile.

"So nice to see you again," said the ginger cat as
he lifted his front leg and licked the sharp looking
claw that extended from his paw. Turning to the
black cats he said, "Is this our dinner approaching?
Shall we eat them now or have some fun?"

"Let's chase them first." said the dirty, black cat.
"I could do with some exercise and I do like a good

chase."

"Tell me, pixies," asked the ginger cat. "Can you run faster than we can?"

"I don't think so," stammered Mitch, reaching out and clutching at Titch for comfort.

By now, the pixies were so frightened and their knees were knocking so loud that the cats could hear them quite clearly.

"Can you climb a tree higher than we can?" the ginger cat sneered and unfurled a claw with which he scratched his chin.

This time there was no answer from the terrified pixies.

"Do you have sharper teeth than we do?"

Still they made no reply.

"Would you like to start running now?" The black cat was eager for his lunch. "I'll bet I catch you first."

All together, the cats leapt at the pixies, claws, teeth and eyes flashing.

Startled at the sight of three cats jumping at him, Mitch crouched down with his arm raised, ready to fend them off. Quick as a flash, Titch grabbed the feather out of Mitch's hat and pointed it at the charging beasts, waggling it as fiercely as he could. A great sparkling light shot out in front of him and, for a moment, he couldn't see the cats at all. Then the sparkles died down and they saw before them the three cats crouched on their bellies with their paws over their eyes, screeching and howling in fright.

They didn't stay like that for long. The ginger cat shouted out, "They are magic pixies, quick we must run." The brothers watched the three wicked cats tumbling down the hillside, falling over each other in their rush to get away.

"Come on Mitch, let's get out of here. I think it's time to leave." Titch sprang towards the magic bicycle, closely followed by Mitch, and moments later, they were flying through the air and away from the hillside.

As they passed over Trusty's cave they called and shouted out goodbye. The Dragon Mouse popped out of his cave and the last thing they saw was a little flash of fire and a white puff of smoke as he waved back.

Follow the further adventures of Titch and Mitch
Volume 2: The Trolls of Sugar Loaf Wood

The Adventures of
Titch & Mitch
The Trolls of
Sugar Loaf Wood

Garth Edwards
Illustrated by Max Stasyuk

Follow the further adventures of Titch and Mitch
Volume 3: The King of the Castle

The Adventures of
Titch & Mitch
The King of the
Castle

Garth Edwards
Illustrated by Max Stasyuk